A DISGUISE

The Untold Story

Author:
Anaya Lee Willabus

Cover Designed By:
Chantelle Teekasingh
&
Anaya Lee Willabus

Photographer: **Chantelle Teekasingh**

SPECIAL THANKS

Firstly, I am very thankful to the Creator for the guidance and blessings in making my dreams a reality of publishing yet, another book.

Secondly, to my wonderful family who has always been there, right by my side, I love you very much.

Thirdly, to all of my friends, supporters, fans and well wishers, I thank you for your continuous support!

Lastly, I look forward to creating many more great memories of which I hope will inspire and motivate others to follow their dreams, too.

Thank You!

Anaya Lee Willabus

Award Winning Author & Poet

Anaya Lee Willabus

CONTENTS

1. The Phone Call   1

2. Friendship   9

3. The Family Function   25

4. The Longest Week of School   42

5. The Day Before   49

6. The Dis "Appointment"   57

7. The Introduction to School   63

8. The Phone Report   74

9. Stand Up for Your Rights   83

10. Forgive and Forget   101

This Book Belongs To

_____

Anaya Lee Willabus

Chapter One - The Phone Call

It was truly a great Spring day! There was the sun, gently warming my skin, a slight breeze blowing, the smell of fresh grass in the air, and even the birds chirping and bees buzzing. This was certainly one of my favorite times of year. Not only was the weather warm and sunny, but I felt good about school. I felt that this was a terrific start to the new semester of fourth grade and I was on track with all of my subjects. One more successful semester and the adventures of summer break would be at hand.

As Grandma Celeste entered the living room, Mohan rushed to hide his sweater. "Boy, did that thing have a huge hole! I could never imagine a pencil point doing such damage!" Mohan thought.

Ring....ring...."Mohan, tell your grandmother to please answer the phone," said Mrs. Singh.

"Ma, she went back upstairs!" yelled Mohan. "Well, if it is that important, whoever it was will call back," Mrs. Singh said as she rushed out of the bathroom towards her phone. "Oh my, Mohan. It was Ms. Gladia, Mona's mom. I wonder what made her call. Let me listen to my voicemail and buzz her back to see what's going on!" Mrs. Singh stormed through the kitchen from the bathroom, into the living room, wiping her hands with a paper napkin, all while hugging her cellular phone under her arm. She called Ms. Gladia and Mohan could hear the happy sounding voice on the other end of the phone.

Anaya Lee Willabus

Mohan knew that this would be the start of a lengthy conversation between Mrs. Singh and Ms. Gladia, as they reminisced and traded some really old time stories. Mohan had heard many of these stories, several times over. Often he felt he could tell the stories himself, as if he had actually lived the experience. Although many of the stories involved him, Mohan could scarcely recall the details, because he was so young at the time of the incidents. This didn't concern Mohan; he was more interested in hearing about Mona, Ms. Gladia's daughter and his old friend. He wondered whether there would be any news of how she was doing back in Smalltown, Georgia or whether the old neighborhood changed. All Mohan could think about was the great days of trying to ride his tricycle with

A Bully's Disguise

Mona and how they enjoyed each other's company. Mrs. Singh finally got off of the phone and explained that Ms. Gladia and Mona would be coming to Brooklyn. "When are they coming to visit? How long will they stay? Will it be for the whole summer?" Mohan inquired. "Calm down, calm down." Mrs. Singh said. She continued, "They are moving here to live and they will need help finding an apartment, a job and a good school for Mona to attend." Mohan was the happiest kid in the world. He didn't know much about finding apartments or work, but he knew exactly where the best school would be for his old friend! He could not recall a happier day than this, in a long time.

"Mom, why don't you have them come by our house to live and Mona can attend PS

1102 with me?" questioned Mohan. "Mohan, I cannot afford to take care of two more people right now," replied Mrs. Singh. "Ok Mom, I understand," said Mohan, looking a bit disappointed. "I will look around for a job for Gladia and an apartment for them," continued Mrs. Singh. "Could you please look in this neighborhood, so that Mona and I can go to the same school?" Mohan asked gently. "Yes Mohan, I will do that!" sighed Mrs. Singh.

Mohan ran swiftly upstairs to his room with his sweater clinched under his arm, trying his best to prevent his mother from noticing the hole.

Mrs. Singh noticed a needle and thread were on the handle of the couch. Though she looked at it puzzled, she simply assumed Grandma Celeste had left it there. Grandma

A Bully's Disguise

Celeste loved to stitch everything in her sight and she was quite the sewing wizard.

Mrs. Singh called up a few of her co-workers from the hospital where she worked and asked if they knew of any vacancies or apartments for rent. Meanwhile, Mohan dropped off his sweater in his room and ran downstairs to find out if there was any good news.

"Mohan, go and get your homework finished up!" said Mrs. Singh.

"Yes ma!" replied Mohan.

Mrs. Singh's phone rang again and it was Meena, one of her co-workers. She had good news. She knew of a few job openings as a home health aide. However, the only problem was that Ms. Gladia would need to be certified in New York. This was something Mrs. Singh was not sure about.

Mrs. Singh called Ms. Gladia and explained the specifics of the job. She explained that Ms. Gladia would need to receive a certification from New York State, since she lived in Georgia and the laws there were different. All of this would delay the hiring process. Ms. Gladia explained that she had some money saved and that she would be willing to get recertified in New York.

"Excellent news Gladia! I will call my friend, Meena, and let her know that you have an interest," said Mrs. Singh.

"Yeaaah...I'm so excited for Mona to come to New York!" said Mohan running around and jumping as though he had ants in his pants! Mohan exclaimed, "This school year is going to be better than I expected! I can't

A Bully's Disguise

wait to tell Collette about Mona. I know they will be so excited to meet each other!"

Mohan ran to sip some water from his cup and as he leaped into the kitchen, Mrs. Singh laughed and shook her head.

"Children, they can be so funny at times," Mrs. Singh mumbled to herself.

"Mohan did you finish your homework?"

"Yes, ma!" yelled Mohan from the kitchen, to his mother.

Chapter Two - Friendship

It was Monday morning and Mohan could not wait to tell Collette about Mona. As he sat on the cheese bus, he could barely compose himself. He looked out the window and imagined how he and Mona would take the bus to and from school and it would be like the old times. The school bus made a sharp turn and all the kids leaned to the right side to prepare for the turn. "If only the cheese bus had better seatbelts, everyone could sit more comfortably," thought Mohan, as he watched some of the other kids pretend to ride the waves of the bumpy school bus ride.

As the school bus pulled up to PS 1102, Mohan saw Collette being dropped off by her dad.

A Bully's Disguise

"Hey, Collette!" yelled Mohan.

As Collette turned around Mohan caught up to her.

"I have some great news to share with you!" Mohan explained.

"What is it, what is it...tell me, tell me!" Collette said as she took off her hat and sweater.

Mohan and Collette sat in the auditorium and started to chat about their weekend. Mohan took off his sweater and placed it in his bag as he started to tell Collette about his friend Mona from Smalltown, Georgia.

Collette looked puzzled as Mohan went on to tell her how great it would be to have Mona as a student at PS 1102.

Anaya Lee Willabus

"That's so nice to hear about your friend. I guess it would be great to have her attend our school," said Collette.

Joseph, one of Mohan's friends, passed by. Mohan went along with him, to chat until it was time to line up. Joseph and Mohan loved to compare facts about new things they both learned during the weekend. Joseph went on to explain about a movie he watched on planets. He added that one day he would like to visit the moon.

Mohan laughed and said, "Good luck with that one!" Mohan continued, "I am fine on Earth and I like to feel the ground. Gravity is my friend."

The boys joined their class line and headed upstairs to the third floor classroom where they would start the new school day.

A Bully's Disguise

Collette tagged along behind with a few of the girls from her class, as they usually do, chatting up a storm on what they did during the weekend.

Ms. Clara, the fourth grade home room teacher waited patiently for everyone to sit and unpack, then she took attendance.

As Mohan looked across to Collette's desk, he recognized that she was drawing something in her notebook. Walter, one of the boys that sat behind Collette started laughing at her drawing.

Walter called out to Mohan, "You have to see what she is drawing!"

"It's a picture of you, Collette and another person, except the person has a weird face," said Walter. Mohan rushed to Collette's table and leaning over her as he peered into her notebook.

"Who is that person that is hanging out with us?" asked Mohan.

Before Collette could respond, Ms. Clara started clapping her hands. This was a class gesture that signaled that it was time for everyone in the class to stop talking and pay attention. This was quite useful since she had such a soft voice. Any time that Ms. Clara tried to speak over the noisy class, it never worked. Ms. Clara discovered that a creative way to signal her desire to the class was through her claps. After she did this, the students stopped talking and paid attention.

"Class, please take out your ELA notebook and pass it up to the front of your row. Today, we will continue to work on a few more effective ways to assist you for your state exams, which will be here before you know it," said Ms. Clara.

Ms. Clara yelled at Collette since she was distracted drawing again in her notebook. This was not like Collette. She was always very focused.

Mohan could not wait until lunch to speak with her on what was going on. Collette was definitely not herself. Mohan could not stop wondering if she had a bad weekend, but chose not to share it. As the minutes turned to hours and lunch was approaching Mr. Bartfort, the school principal, came into Mohan's class and called him to do a job. Mohan slapped his face and looked up to the ceiling. He was counting the time down to lunch and now he wasn't sure if he would be back in time to catch up with Collette. Mohan packed up his belongings and headed out the door with Mr. Bartfort. Mohan went to the main office to collect a few envelopes which needed be distributed to various teachers. He rushed down the hallway as fast as he could, but the security guard called him back.

"Hello mister, where do you think you are going with all that speed?" asked Mrs. Wilson.

She was the most serious security guard at the school. In her spare time, which appeared to be all day, she patrolled the hallways as though it was a military compound, full of top secret information. Once she was in a good mood, she would share with students, a few good stories of her upbringing in Jamaica. The older students knew that it was better to stand at the side of her just to avoid the remnants of the peanuts that she chewed which were being 'spit out' during her juicy conversations. While Mrs. Wilson spoke to Mohan, he could hear the footsteps from the children coming down for lunch. Mrs. Wilson told Mohan to hurry along without running.

"Oh no, don't tell me it's time for lunch already! I gotta get my act together and rush these envelopes off," thought Mohan.

As Mohan hurried along to do his job, his class went off to the cafeteria for their lunch break.

The scene in the cafeteria was a predictable setting. As usual, the boys were squished together talking about their video games and Mindcraft, while the girls were huddled gossiping about fashion, music and the latest entertainment news.

Mohan ran into the cafeteria as everyone else was finishing up their lunch. He went to sit with the boys, but there was no space. Joseph got up and gave Mohan a chance to sit and eat. Mohan gobbled his food down in a couple of minutes. His stomach grumbled like a storm was about to unleash its wrath. As Mohan finished chewing his last bite, he ran behind Collette through the double doors which led to the school playground.

"Collette, what's going on with you? You are acting strange. Is everything okay?" asked Mohan.

"I'm fine! Why do you care anyway?" replied Collette.

"What in the world are you talking about?" inquired Mohan. "Just tell me what is going on. You seemed to be fine this morning," Mohan said, puzzled by Collette's actions.

Collette got up and ran her usual laps around the school yard as Mohan tried to walk at the side of her.

"Don't worry about me, I'm good!" said Collette.

"Whatever!" said Mohan.

Mohan ran off to hang out with Joseph and Walter. The boys usually walked with their soccer ball, basketball or football to school, so that they could play during recess. Mohan loved to show off his dribbling skills with the soccer ball. He used the school yard as a practice session since he was not always able to attend soccer practice after school because of homework or his soccer schedule conflicting with his mom's job.

"Hey, Mohan, not bad, but check out these moves!" said Walter.

Mohan laughed as Walter tried to perform a few soccer tricks of his own. Ms. Anita and Ms. George started to call the students to line up. It was time to head back in from lunch.

"I wish the school day inside would speed by as quickly as it does outside!" said Joseph.

Collette tried to avoid Mohan and rushed to the start of the line. Mohan stayed to the back with his other friends, Joseph and Walter.

"One day we may be stung by one of those bees," said Mohan with a concerned facial expression. He gestured toward a tree that stood along the center of the schoolyard.

A Bully's Disguise

Within the tree was a beehive that the students and staff knew all too well.

"We have been hanging out on that bench for the longest while. If we trouble the bees, then we have to worry. You know we only sit there because everyone avoids that space due to the fear of being stung," said Walter.

"True, true. I am sweating like a pig!" said Joseph.

"Dude, pigs don't sweat..but you do smell like one!" Walter said, laughing.

Mohan took out his napkin from his pocket to wipe the sweat from his face and before he could throw it out Walter asked for it.

"Yo, that's nasty. Why do you want his stinky, sweaty napkin?" asked Joseph.

Joseph ran off to catch up with the line. All the while, he was laughing. Mohan told Walter it was better to wipe his face on his own shirt than to borrow someone else's napkin.

The school day was coming to an end and Mohan's class went off to the computer lab.

"I don't like group projects," mumbled Regina, another student in Mohan's class.

"Well, I guess you will have a tough life!" replied Walter.

"What are you trying to say?" asked Regina.

"Just facts, just facts. In life you will have to deal with others to get a task done," said Walter.

"Let me worry about adulthood when I

get there, not now!" said Regina.

"You missed my point Regina," Walter said.

Mohan glanced at the time and remembered that his grandmother would be picking him up from school with Uncle Ravin. They were going to visit Queens, in order to participate in a religious Hindu function. Mohan went through his bag to see whether he had any additional snacks, since the drive to Queens would take some time and everyone would have to wait until the religious function was done, to eat.

"Oh great, no snacks! Now I have to deal with this rumbling stomach, again." thought Mohan.

As the time approached for dismissal, the class grew anxious and everyone started to pack up prematurely. Mr. Noel, the computer teacher, stopped everyone in their tracks.

"Hello everyone, you still have ten more minutes to work on your group projects. Use your time wisely since most of you are not even half way done!" said Mr. Noel.

"Ha, ha, ha...good for all of you! What's the rush to leave here anyway?" asked Walter.

"To leave, some of us like our home!" said Joseph.

"Who told you I don't like my home? My mom sends me to after school because she works late," said Walter.

"Okay kids, you may leave now, " said Mr. Noel.

Mr. Noel was one of the most favored teachers. He was cool and all the kids enjoyed his class. He had a liberal mindset and didn't

A Bully's Disguise

believe in punishing kids. He expressed himself well through his teachings and dress code. When switching classrooms for computer, some of the girls wondered what Mr. Noel's next outfit would be. It was always SCREAMING bright. Today, was no different. He wore his tight red corduroy pants and a bright green shirt. Mr. Noel watched as Mohan scrambled through his backpack and asked Mohan if he was missing something. Mohan continued to search while walking towards the door, but there were no snacks.

Uncle Ravin pulled up to the curb to collect Mohan. Ms. Clara told Mohan he could go, since she saw his grandmother waving her hands.

Chapter 3 - The Family Function

Grandma Celeste asked Mohan how his day was and he replied by saying it was good. Uncle Ravin was the only brother of Mohan's dad and Grandma Celeste's only living child.

"Uncle, what time is the jhandi?" Mohan asked.

"It should start around 5 pm and finish at about 5:45 pm," replied Uncle Ravin.

Mohan wasn't sure that he could survive not being able to eat for such a long time. He was already hungry and on a typical day, he'd arrive home via the cheese bus at 3:15 pm. His mother or grandmother would be finished cooking by that time and he would be able to sit down to a nice hot meal! Today, his routine was in disarray.

A Bully's Disguise

As Mohan sat in the car, the highway traffic seemed to be at a standstill. Mohan could only focus on one thing, food.

"Take out your notebook and start your homework, don't wait for me to tell you everything, boy!" Grandma Celeste said sternly. "Yes, Grandma!" replied Mohan.

Uncle Ravin and Grandma Celeste started their usual old time conversation, which helped Mohan learn a lot about his family's history. He eavesdropped while trying to do his homework.

Grandma Celeste started talking about when Mohan's dad, Mr. Dayal Singh, and Uncle Ravin were children.

"The two of you were funny little things," Grandma Celeste laughed as she drifted down memory lane.

"I remembered how the two of you would fight and play, all day long. Time is truly powerful," Grandma Celeste added.

"Yep, those days we can't get back. All we can do is try to give our children the best life possible," replied Uncle Ravin.

"During a jhandi back in Guyana, you and your brother were my helpers. I could count on the two of you to help in cutting up the vegetables for the seven curries and even sweeping and washing the back yard," Grandma Celeste went on.

"I remember helping to do those things," laughed Uncle Ravin.

"Why do they call the food 'seven curries', anyway?" asked Mohan.

Grandma Celeste loved to talk about her rich Guyanese culture. She went on to tell

A Bully's Disguise

Mohan that during a jhandi , a Hindu religious function, neither meat nor 'rank' foods are served, but different vegetables are cooked as substitutes. Some preferred vegetables are curried, like: chick peas, potatoes, pumpkin, callaloo, katahar and eggplant. All of these different curries are usually served with white rice and dhal, which is similar to gravy, but made of split peas. Grandma Celeste went on to explain that in Guyana the food was served in a huge lily pad-type leaf and everyone ate with their hands.

"Also, when the chutney music came on, we were the first to hit the dance floor," Uncle Ravin added.

"Ha, ha, ha! Yes, you boys had your father's dance moves," added Grandma Celeste.

Anaya Lee Willabus

Mohan sat in the back seat listening to the conversation while trying to understand the music that his uncle played on the radio. He could never understand why his uncle listened to music in the Hindi language, but could neither speak nor interpret what was being played.

"Uncle, those songs have a really good beat, but what are they saying?" asked Mohan.

"Son, I don't know, but I do know that I grew up on this genre of music and listening to it has become a habit. Not to mention, you can't argue that the beat is quite catchy!" said Uncle Ravin.

"True, true, I like the sound of the beats," added Mohan.

Mohan sat his notebook on his lap and peered through the car window, trying to ascertain whether the traffic was moving faster.

"This time of the day is 'rush hour', there's nothing we can do but listen to some music and chat!" went on Uncle Ravin.

Mohan did not worry about what time he got to Queens. He knew that he was almost finished with his homework and he always made the claim that he could smell Queens, just before getting there. The rich whiff of curry mixed with other spices teased the nose as you get closer.

"Grandma, what is a jhandi?" asked Mohan.

"It is a prayer service dedicated to the Hindu gods," replied Grandma Celeste.

"Hmm, but how am I a Christian?" asked Mohan puzzled.

"Well, your mother is a Christian and your father chose to live that life since he met your mom, which is perfectly fine child. After you were born, you were baptized in a church," said Grandma Celeste.

"Okay, that sounds confusing to keep up with!" said Mohan.

"No, it is not confusing. You are blessed to have a family that includes different religions and everyone is okay with it, NOW!" Grandma Celeste replied.

"When I was young, you could not marry out of your religion. The old time folks did not believe in a lot of things that happen today, but that's how it is when times changes my boy," continued Grandma Celeste.

Oh, it was that whiff that had Mohan turning his head. He could smell the alluring aroma of spices and food.

"Hey, we are about to reach uncle!" said Mohan with an excited tone of voice.

"Sit down Mohan and keep your seat belt on," Uncle Ravin said.

Mohan thought of the cheese bus and how he and his school mates would lean to the side grabbing their battered up seat belts for dear life as the bus turned, but it wasn't the same in his uncle's car. The seat belt actually braced him into his seat, not allowing for the rush he was hoping for.

Mohan, Uncle Ravin and Grandma Celeste got out of the car and went into the one family, two-story house. The music was loud and everyone was yelling at each other instead of speaking in a normal tone. Mohan was accustomed to the loud music since Uncle

Ravin was known for being a music lover. It was nearly 4 pm, the food was ready and Mohan's stomach was aching for nourishment. Mohan was considering an attempt to sneak off to the corner store to grab a bite. He knew the food was not to be eaten until the pandit, the Hindu scholar and teacher, prayed over it.

Mohan checked his pocket and remembered that he had a single dollar left, from a few days ago, which was being saved for hard times. Certainly, this situation qualified as a tough time. He snuck out of the back door and ran up the block to the corner store. Mohan found out that the cheapest candy bar or chips were one dollar and twenty five cents.

"Oh great!" Mohan exhaled with frustration. He could not believe he needed twenty five more cents. Mohan stood outside the store and looked around with the hope that someone had dropped coins from the laundromat across the street. While he stood there, one of the neighbors passed by and recognized Mohan.

"Hello there young man, what are you doing, hanging out here? Aren't you Ms. Celeste's grandson?" asked the neighbor.

"Yes, madam!" replied Mohan with fear in his voice.

"I am waiting on my grandmother. She went to get something and will be back soon," replied Mohan.

"Oh, okay," said the neighbor.

"That was a close one. I should have asked her if she had a quarter," whispered Mohan.

Mohan went back into the store and asked the store attendant if she could please sell him the candy bar or a pack of chips for a dollar. He went on to explain his situation and the lady was nice enough to sell him a candy bar for one dollar. Mohan ran back down the block to Uncle Ravin's house as he chewed as fast as he could. His mouth had to be empty before getting there.

Mohan ran inside and reached for his water bottle from his backpack and washed his mouth out. He was truly happy for a few minutes, until Grandma Celeste showed up and asked where he was. He explained that he went outside to get some fresh air and to look around the neighborhood.

"You know very well that I expect you to tell me if you leave this house!" Grandma

A Bully's Disguise

Celeste said with her hands on her hip.

"Yes, Grandma. I'm sorry," replied Mohan.

"Don't move out of my sight again, boy," said Grandma Celeste.

Mohan shook his head and sat down on the floor where his aunt laid bed sheets for her guests to sit for the jhandi. It was a custom for everyone to sit with their legs like a pretzel. Mohan could never get it right but he always tried. His legs would cramp up and he would have to hop to the patio for a while during the service.

Grandma Celeste called out to Mohan and told him to sit towards the back of the crowd, so that if he needed to get up, he would not disturb anyone else.

The service started a few minutes late and Mohan was still preoccupied with the thought of the food. He was thinking of how he would have to wait a few minutes past six to eat a really late lunch, or dinner, in this case.

"I will not need to get up during the service, but I will sit to the back," thought Mohan.

Mohan watched, just like all the other children, how the pandit prayed over the food and laid flowers at the feet of the gods.

"Mohan, what happened to your leg? Why is it stretched out so much?" Grandma Celeste asked.

"It's all cramped up Grandma!" Mohan responded.

Grandma Celeste called Mohan outside to sit until the jhandi was done.

A Bully's Disguise

"That's why I told you to sit at the back, because I know you," said Grandma Celeste.

Mohan could hear the adults moving around in the kitchen. It was an indication that the late lunch was about to be served.

"Finally, it's time to eat!" said Mohan.

Mohan ate as though he never had food before. There was a permanent smile plastered on his face as he devoured a variety of traditional foods. Grandma Celeste had to stop him from asking for more food.

"Mohan do not overstuff your stomach!" Grandma Celeste said.

After a few minutes, everyone was finished eating. The usual conversations ensued about how school and work was going. Also, the adults were chatting about who died from the last time they saw each other.

Anaya Lee Willabus

All Mohan could see was Grandma Celeste storming through the crowd on her phone.

"Mohan, did you remember to call your mom, after school, to let her know you were okay?" asked Grandma Celeste.

"I'm sorry, I forgot!" replied Mohan.

Mohan took the phone from Grandma Celeste and spoke with his mom. His mom's voice hinted of concern and frustration, since it was a house rule that he must call her once he was home or otherwise. He apologized to his mom and told her that they would be heading back to Brooklyn soon.

Mohan said his goodbyes to family and friends and headed to Uncle Ravin's car with his grandmother.

Mohan was so happy to return home.

A Bully's Disguise

He ran into the shower and hopped into bed shortly thereafter.

"Can you tell me how these holes got into your sweater, mister?" asked Grandma Celeste.

"Aaahhh...I was playing around with my pencil, at school," replied Mohan.

"You'd better appreciate everything you have, because there are lots of children who do not have anything," continued Grandma Celeste.

"Yes, Grandma," said Mohan.

Mrs. Singh came into Mohan's room to say goodnight. She also asked about his sweater and agreed with Grandma Celeste.

"It is important to take care of what you have and not destroy it. Say your prayers and get some rest," continued Mrs. Singh.

Mrs. Singh tucked Mohan in and just as he finished saying his prayer, Mohan asked his mom if she had heard from Mona's mom.

"Actually, Mona and Gladia will be in New York by this weekend," Mrs. Singh said.

Mohan popped his head back up with a bright face.

"Really, I am so excited for this weekend to come!" Mohan said.

"Go to sleep now, Mohan," Mrs. Singh replied.

Mohan lay on his bed with his two hands under his pillow as he looked up to the ceiling. All he could think of was the countdown to the weekend.

A Bully's Disguise

Chapter 4 - The Longest Week of School

It was Tuesday and for Mohan it felt as if the week was not moving fast enough. All he could think about was Mona and her move to Brooklyn. He was happy that his mom was able to assist Mona and her mom to locate an apartment close to where he lived, so that he and Mona could travel on the bus, to and from school. Mohan dropped his backpack on the floor beside his desk and slumped over to chat with Lulu. She was in Mohan's karate class. They both practiced Shotokan karate, which was the Japanese martial art that meant, "empty hand". Lulu and Mohan received notices to test for new karate belts. Success in the test would make Mohan a 2nd degree, brown belt and Lulu a first degree, brown belt.

The two chatted for a few minutes before Collette came into class.

"Good morning, Collette!" Mohan said.

"Good morning!" Collette replied with an upset face.

Mohan could not figure out what was wrong with Collette. She had been ignoring him and he could not figure out the reason. In order to not upset Collette further, Mohan asked Lulu if she would be willing to chat with Collette during lunch, in order to figure out what was making her act in such an unusual way. Lulu agreed.

Ms. Clara came into the class and everyone went quiet for a few minutes. Mohan could hear Walter and Collette whispering. Mohan did not want to turn around for fear that he may get into trouble so he batted his ear to listen. After taking the attendance, the students were instructed by Ms. Clara to retrieve their library books from within their desks and to begin independently reading. Mohan used this opportunity to turn around and find out what Walter and Collette were talking about.

Again, she was drawing more pictures of strange characters!

"I do not think she likes the idea of sharing your friendship with your friend from Georgia," Walter stated to Mohan.

"Don't be silly, we are all friends in this class," Mohan replied.

"Now, who gave you the right to make such an assumption, Walter?" Collette asked.

"If I choose to draw or stop speaking with someone, that's my choice!"

Collette went on.

Mohan quietly went back to his seat without seeing the drawing that Walter kept talking about.

The day could not drag on any slower for Mohan. He brought a PB & J sandwich, his favorite, for lunch and was looking forward to destroying that sandwich in a hurry!

After lunch, Mohan, Walter and Joseph went to the usual hang out spot on the bench, under the bee nested tree.

"What do you have planned for this weekend, Joseph?" asked Walter.

"I have to go with my family to church on Sunday, but I am free on Saturday, after my chores are done." Joseph replied.

"Okay, so we can hang out at my place and play some games?" asked Walter.

A Bully's Disguise

"That's cool!" said Joseph.

"Wait a minute, what about me? Neither of you asked me what I was doing! What's up with that?" asked Mohan.

"Well, we know you are expecting your friend from Georgia. That's all you have been talking about, so we assumed you would not have time to hang out with us." said Walter.

Mohan could not say a word.

"Fine, you got me! I can't hang out this weekend, but I can for sure next week," said Mohan.

Lulu came running towards the boys as they lined up to head back in from the school yard.

"Mohan, you are on your own! Collette doesn't want to talk about you," Lulu said.

Mohan did not reply. He just shook his

head as he walked in line back to class.

Joseph had gotten himself a new watch, so every five minutes, the class got a time check.

Mohan was kind of happy, since he was rushing the week through. Everyone teased Joseph about his new watch. Every chance that a classmate had, they would ask Joseph, "what time is it?" and he would happily oblige them with a smile and flick of his watch-studded wrist.

The end of the day was approaching with one class left, Art. Most of the children did not mind Art, since it was an escape from the usual ELA or Math state test preparations. While they knew it was in their best interest, the children got a bit overwhelmed sometimes. Ms. Trudy, the Art teacher, had an interesting

A Bully's Disguise

personality. She would speak as though she was singing aloud, while in class. Everyone replied with a similar tone, making the last class of the day feel like a breeze.

Mohan spaced out. As he packed away his stuff and hung his artwork on the board, he mentally counted the days until Mona 's arrival.

Chapter 5 - The Day Before

A few days had past and it was at about 5 am, that Friday morning, when Mrs. Singh heard Mohan coughing from his room across the hall. She got up and went to his room to check on him. Mohan had a slight temperature. Mrs. Singh was a bit worried so she woke up Grandma Celeste. Grandma Celeste had the cure for everything! She got a rag and a small bowl and went to Mohan's room. She began to dip the rag into the bowl of cold water and placed it on Mohan's forehead. He quickly jumped out of his sleep and looked around. He saw his mom and grandmother and knew why they were in his room, so he lay back on his bed with his eyes closed. Grandma Celeste continued to apply the cold compress to Mohan's head until he was not so warm anymore. Mrs. Singh told Mohan to sit up and she gave him some medicine. Mohan went back to sleep.

Mohan awoke to sound of voices. His bedroom door was always remained slightly open. In the case of an emergency, it would be easier for his mom to hear him. Mohan sprang up and checked the time. It was 9:15 am! He jumped out of his bed and ran into the bathroom to take a shower to rush to school. His mom stopped him and told him that it was okay, to go back to bed. She took the day off to ensure he was better and she wanted him to rest some more.

"It was that soccer game that got you sick, boy! You have to walk with a change of clothes if you are going to play a game in the rain," said Grandma Celeste.

"I did wear a hat, but the rain was falling too hard for the hat to help," replied Mohan.

Mohan remembered that Mona was supposed to arrive from Georgia. He was waiting for such a long time! Mrs. Singh refused to answer any questions on Mona until Mohan went to bed and rested some more. Mohan went back to his room and lay there feeling a bit cold and hungry. He thought it might have been better to have breakfast, then go back to bed, so he called his grandmother and shared his idea. She agreed and made him blueberry pancakes with eggs and orange juice. Mohan ran back to bed after eating.

Ms. Gladia and Mona did arrive, but they went directly to their new apartment. They arrived to New York a day early, so that Ms.

A Bully's Disguise

Gladia could take care of Mona's paperwork for school, before her first day.

At around 5 pm, Mohan asked his mom if he could talk to her about Mona and she responded, not until his homework was done. Mohan called Walter on his cellular phone and asked him to provide the information for the missed day's work. Walter told Mohan that he was missed at school and that he would pass by his house, after his mom picked him up from his after-school program.

Sure enough, Walter kept his word and passed by around 6:30 pm with a few sheets of class work.

"Remember to do the essay on page 235 and answer the short answers," said Walter.

"Thanks for stopping by," said Mohan.

"You have to stop playing so many

sports and be tough like me," Walter told Mohan.

"Ha, ha, ha... yeah right! You're only tough with words, not sports, Walter! After all, I mainly play two sports, soccer and karate. That's not too much! Besides, if I had the opportunity, I would learn more. It is good to know different sports. My dad always told me to never stop playing sports." Mohan went on.

"Okay, I hear you, Mohan!" Walter replied. "But, remember super-athlete, I'm the tough guy that had to bring your school work to you." The two friends shared a chuckle.

Walter said his goodbyes and left. The boys agreed to see each other in school soon. Mohan rushed inside and started his homework.

Mrs. Singh was watching "Little Big

A Bully's Disguise

Shots" with Grandma Celeste as Mohan joined
them in the living room.

"Is Mona in New York yet?" Mohan
asked in a gentle voice.

"Yes, Mohan. We have to give them
time to settle in. We MAY go to see them
tomorrow, providing you are feeling better,"
Mrs. Singh replied.

"Yes, ma. I will definitely feel better!"
Mohan said.

Mrs. Singh explained that Ms. Gladia had
a lot of things to get done and it would be
intrusive to just show up at someone's
apartment unannounced. Mohan felt as
though he had waited so long to see Mona and
the time was not moving fast enough. Mrs.
Singh's cellular phone rang and, as she
answered, she looked at Mohan.

It was Mona using her mom's phone to speak with Mohan.

"Hi , Mona. Are you okay?" asked Mohan.

"Yes, I am fine, I can't wait to see you and to start school on Monday!" said Mona.

"Me, too!" said Mohan.

As Mohan spoke with Mona, he continued to cough. Mrs. Singh told him to wrap up his conversation and he did. Mrs. Singh told Mohan that if he was not feeling better by the next day, she would be forced to take him to the doctor. Mohan did not want to hear that at all, but he agreed. She told him to go back to bed after watching "Little Big Shots" and eating dinner. Mohan thought to himself that it was going to be a long night and weekend, but he was looking forward to seeing

A Bully's Disguise

his old friend, Mona, the next day.

Mohan hopped off to bed and said his prayers as his mom and grandmother tucked him in.

"Tonight, you have your mom, you don't need me!" Grandma Celeste said with a little chuckle.

"I always need you Grandma!" Mohan replied.

"That's my boy! Well, I am going to always be here for you. I promised your dad, that I will make sure you are well taken care of," said Grandma Celeste as she walked off.

Mohan gazed at the ceiling, wondering what interesting new things the next day would bring . He thought it best to sleep, so that time would move faster and his body could feel better after a good night's rest.

Chapter 6 - The Dis "Appointment"

It was Saturday morning and Mohan was still not better. Mrs. Singh had already taken two days off from work to take care of Mohan and only had one more day to spare. She told him that she had made an appointment with his pediatrician and he had to go, regardless of how much he did not want to go.

"What about Mona? How am I going to see her, if I have to go to the doctor?" whined Mohan.

"Little boy, you are going to do as you are told! We had an agreement. You are not fully recovered and you will have a lot of time to see Mona in school," said Mrs. Singh.

Mohan dragged himself to his room, got ready and left with his mom for the doctor's office. The doctor told Mrs. Singh that Mohan had a temperature and it was a common symptom of the flu. However, as a precaution, he would not be able to attend school for a few days, so that he did not spread anything to his peers.

When Mohan heard the news, he was devastated. Mohan cried so hard, not for having the flu, but to know he would not be able to leave home for a few days while Mona was in town.

"Ma, is there any way Mona can visit me?" Mohan asked, with tears running down his face.

"No, that would not be a good idea. When you feel better, all of your friends can visit," replied Mrs. Singh.

Mrs. Singh and Mohan's drive home was

the quietest ever! He sat in the back of the car like a sad puppy that had lost its owner. Mrs. Singh gave him a quick peek, every now and again from the rear view mirror, just to ensure he was okay.

When they got home, Mohan ran into the house and went straight to his bed. Grandma Celeste was not having that kind of behavior. She called him downstairs.

"Where do you get off coming in here without greeting me, when I am sitting right in front of you? Get over yourself and remember your manners!" Grandma Celeste said.

"Yes, Madam, I am sorry!" replied Mohan.

"How was the doctor's visit? Is everything okay?" Grandma Celeste inquired.

"He said that I have the flu and that I will

need to stay away from everyone for about a week!" Mohan exclaimed.

"I'm truly sorry to hear that, boy. I know it will be rough, but we'll make the best of it. I'll try to see what remedies I can cook up to help you get up and about, as soon as, possible," Grandma Celeste said reassuringly.

"Thanks, Grandma," Mohan responded, as he retreated to his room.

Mohan went back to his room and lay there until his mom called him. She told him that Walter had called to see how he was doing. Mohan's face lit up for a few minutes.

"Hey there, how are you feeling? I guess I will see you at school on Monday?" asked Walter.

"No, I am afraid NOT!" replied Mohan.

Mohan went on to explain that he had

the flu and would not be able to attend school for a few days. Walter told him that he can ask his mom to bring by the homework and school work daily. Mohan explained that his mom had emailed Ms. Clara and she agreed to email the missed class work and homework.

The boys continued to chat and Walter agreed to pass by another day to see how Mohan was doing. Mohan went on to explain to Walter that Mona would be starting PS 1102 on Monday. He asked his friend to assist Mona with whatever she needed to make her transition to her new school seamless. Walter agreed and said he would do his best to show Mona around.

Mohan asked his mom to call Mona. She agreed and the two children chatted for a while. Mohan told Mona about his friends and explained that Walter will show her around. He was not going to mention Collette until Mona asked for her.

"Oh, Collette...you will see her there, too." said Mohan.

"Should I ask her to show me around since that is your friend, too?" asked Mona.

"Ah...well, just ask Walter for now," said Mohan with a doubtful voice.

Mona was a little confused, since Mohan always talked so much about Collette. Mona wanted to meet Collette so badly. She envisioned that she would have a strong bond with Collette, just like with Mohan.

Mohan told Mona that he had to get off the phone, so they ended the conversation with hopes of seeing each other soon.

Anaya Lee Willabus

Chapter 7 - The Introduction to School

A sunny Monday morning rolled around and Mona was so excited to start school. She hadn't had the opportunity to see her long-time friend since arriving to Brooklyn, but she was happy to know that she was attending the same school as Mohan. Ms. Gladia took Mona to school with a taxi, since it was her first day and she wanted to see her off without any troubles. Mona kissed her mom and went into the auditorium.

Collette was already in school, so she went up to Mona and introduced herself. The two girls seemingly got along, just fine. Collette treated Mona so kindly that Mona went on to tell her how Mohan spoke highly of their friendship. Collette smiled and said,

A Bully's Disguise

"That was nice of Mohan."

At around 7:50 am Walter arrived. He walked into the auditorium and saw the girls chatting happily. He quickly discerned Mona's identity based on Mohan's description of her, as well as, the fact that she was the only strange person sitting where the class huddled, daily. At 8 am, the lines formed and everyone went to their respected classrooms. Ms. Clara introduced Mona. Mona was very shy and felt a little out of place, but did her best to adapt to her new school, class and classmates. She introduced herself to the class and was warmly received. Mona's big brown eyes lit up as she felt the love from everyone. Collette had saved a seat for Mona next to her.

Just before lunch, Lulu went to show Mona where the bathroom was and as the girls reached the door, they saw a few girls who hung out with Collette, leaving the bathroom, laughing and looking at Mona. Mona and Lulu were very confused until they entered the bathroom. The two girls discovered that someone had posted a drawing of what appeared to be a "welcome sign" for Mona, but as an insult.

The Flyer read:

"GO BACK TO GEORGIA, COUNTRY FOWL!"

The drawing was of a little girl, dressed like a chicken, with an oversized head. Lulu tried to stretch to pull the drawing down but could not reach. It had to be someone who was tall enough to reach that high. Even on their tippy toes the girls could not reach the drawing. Mona started crying and ran out of the bathroom. Lulu jumped and jumped until she could grab a piece of the flyer and finally tore it down. She ran out of the bathroom to catch up with Mona, but Mona had already returned to the classroom. Mona sat with a straight face, trying to hide her dismay. Lulu threw the drawing into the trash on her way to class. Mona was watching her hands to see if she still had the drawing.

During lunch, Lulu and Mona were interrupted by Collette. Collette took Mona to a different table to eat, away from Lulu. Mona wanted to know why Collette moved away from Lulu. Collette asked Mona, "Why do you look so upset?" Mona responded that it was nothing. Collette pressed the issue that something seemed wrong and tried to get Mona to express her feelings. Mona held out and continued to say nothing was wrong. The girls ate their lunch as Walter came up to the table.

"Hi, Mona. Mohan said I should show you around the school," Walter said.

"Hi, yes..he told me about you as well!" replied Mona.

Mona got up and started to walk off into the school yard. Collette jumped up and went behind them. Joseph came along and wanted to hang out with Walter, but Walter told him not today, since he had to show Mona around.

"How much of the school yard is there to see Walter?" asked Joseph.

"School yard meet Mona from Georgia, Mona meet the school yard of PS 1102," continued Joseph.

"Very funny, Joseph!" replied Walter.

A Bully's Disguise

Walter decided that Joseph was telling the truth, that every school yard looked fairly similar, so the boys ran off to play basketball.

Collette used the opportunity to take Mona walking around the track. After a few times around the track, Mona got tired. Mona pointed to the lone vacant bench, under a shaded tree. Collette agreed for Mona to go and sit on the bench. Collette gave Mona a paper fan to walk with to cool down. Mona walked briskly across the school yard and to the bench as Collette kept her eyes on her. Mona asked Collette if she wanted to join her to take a rest, but Collette declined with a grin. Mona sat down and started to fan herself from the heat and aroused the bees that lurked in that tree, which everyone avoided, except the newbie. As Mona continued to fan, the bees came out and surrounded her like honey on a beehive. All the kids in the school yard started to run inside for cover. Walter and Joseph went for Ms. Anita. Mona began screaming at the top of her lungs. Those bees were in an exceptionally ornery mood and buzzed about feverishly. Walter and Joseph dashed into the school building to avoid being stung. Ms. Anita and Ms. George ran toward Mona, helplessly swatting at bees. Mr. Bartfort, the principal, hustled along to close the opened windows and doors and announced over the school intercom that the teachers should do the same. All the kids were talking about Mona and the bees. They were scared!

Walter and Joseph wanted to know what had happened to Mona. They heard the sirens and knew that Mona was probably rushed to the hospital. That brought some relief to the boys.

Lulu sat in the classroom, quietly wondering whether the bee experience was an accident or something planned. Although she had her suspicions, Lulu kept her thoughts to herself. Walter and Joseph were chatting about what a bad first day Mona was having and Lulu told them about the drawing on the bathroom wall. The boys were really shocked and could not figure out who would be so mean.

Collette kept her head in her book and avoided the conversation. Walter tapped Collette on her shoulder and asked her what exactly happened to trigger the bees. Collette explained that Mona wanted to sit under the shaded tree and she warned her about the bees but she insisted on going there anyway. Walter looked at Collette with a strange gaze as she spoke and for some reason Walter did not believe Collette's story.

Ms. Clara came into the class and explained that Mona would be okay. She was rushed to the emergency room having suffered a few bee stings. Everyone was so quiet in the class that Ms. Clara did not have to clap. Lulu was so upset, she could hardly compose herself. She whispered to Walter that the two of them needed to speak after school.

A few hours later, the dismissal bell sounded and Lulu and Walter stood by the school's front door. Lulu told Walter that she believed that Collette set up Mona to be stung by the bees and that the drawing in the bathroom was possibly one drawn by Collette.

A Bully's Disguise

Walter got upset with Lulu.

"How dare you blame Collette for doing that!" said Walter.

"Why are you representing Collette?" asked Lulu.

"I know that Collette would never bully someone. Collette is not that type of person. I have known her for years and she would never harm anyone! Besides, she warned Mona about the bees," said Walter.

"I think she is jealous of Mohan having another close friend. I also think, Collette feels as though Mona would be replacing her," continued Lulu.

Walter walked back into the cafeteria where the after-school kids were, leaving Lulu at the door. Lulu shook her head, thinking that perhaps she was mistaken. As she stood at the pick-up area, waiting for her mother to arrive, Lulu surmised that Monday can truly be a tough start of the week, especially in a new environment, surrounded by unfamiliar faces.

Walter wondered how he could possibly explain to Mohan all the things that happened to Mona on her first day of school. Walter was supposed to call Mohan to find out how he was feeling and to possibly pass by to pay him a visit.

Walter sat in the lunch room with the after-school kids and finished his homework. He was trying to burn time until his mom arrived to pick him up from school. All the while, his brain was scattered, wondering what he might tell Mohan about the events of the day.

A Bully's Disguise

Chapter 8 - The Phone Report

Walter got home around 7 pm and his mom hurried him to take a shower and have dinner. Walter asked his mom if he could call Mohan first, since he wanted to know how his friend was feeling.

"Did something happen in school today, Walter? You were so quiet, that for the first time, I actually missed your usual, 'talk my head off' conversation!" said Walter's mom.

"Ah, no mom!" Walter replied with his head down.

Walter rushed to take a shower and while having his dinner he tried to think of the best words to use to explain the misfortunes which Mona encountered on her first day at PS 1102.

Finally, Walter mustered up enough courage to call Mohan.

"Hey, Mohan, good night! How are you feeling?" asked Walter, sounding hyper.

"I feel so much better today, no more fever. I cannot wait to head back to school tomorrow. Also, all of us can hang out and show Mona around school, so that she does not feel sad or left out being the newbie. How was her first day, anyhow? Did you like her?" asked Mohan.

Walter took a deep breath and scratched his head before responding.

"Well, to tell you the truth Mohan, she did not have such a good first day," said Walter, in a low tone of voice.

"What is THAT suppose to mean?" asked Mohan.

A Bully's Disguise

"She fell on some bad luck," replied Walter.

"Walter, just explain to me what exactly happened, please!" said Mohan.

"Mona was badly stung by the bees at our hang out spot, by the bench. Someone also jokingly posted a flyer in the girl's bathroom about her," Walter went on.

"Tell me that this is a sick prank you are trying to pull!" said Mohan.

Walter and Mohan went on for a few more minutes with their conversation. Mohan was fully informed by Walter of all the things that he had missed, including his homework, even though Ms. Clara had already emailed Mrs. Singh about Mohan's homework.

Anaya Lee Willabus

After observing Mohan getting off the phone with Walter, Grandma Celeste summoned Mohan to sit next to her. She had been overhearing their conversation. She told him one of her old time stories of when she was a little girl. One of her classmates was bullied. "She wore an old uniform to school at the beginning of the school year when everyone else wore their best. The children teased Rani so much that she didn't want to go to school," Grandma Celeste explained.

"What ended up happening?" Mohan anxiously asked.

"Well, she found a way to persevere, in spite of those bullies. She studied so hard that her grades made her excel above everyone in our class, including me," continued Grandma Celeste. "Rani had to tutor many of the children in our class, some of whom, were the bullying children. She did so, without malice. These very children had to decide whether to continue to be bullies or to become true friends to Rani," Grandma Celeste said.

"What did they decide?" Mohan anxiously inquired.

"Well, each child had to choose his own path. However, Rani continued to succeed and she developed relationships with some, once she realized that she could only control the actions of one person: herself. " Grandma Celeste concluded.

"How is that going to help Mona, though?" asked Mohan puzzled.

"My child, what is the purpose of school? Is it to socialize, dress your best or to earn an education?" asked Grandma Celeste.

"Hmm....definitely to earn an education," Mohan responded.

Mohan and Grandma Celeste continued their conversation as Mohan tried to figure out how best to approach the next school day. He wondered if he would be forced to create enemies with current friends, by representing an old friendship.

"Tough decisions are needed sometimes in life my child, let your heart and conscience be your guide," said Grandma Celeste.

Mohan asked his grandmother if it was okay to call Mona. He was anxious to find out, from her, what her perspective was of the day's events. Upon Grandma Celeste's approval, Mohan called Ms Gladia. She sounded very upset and did not allow Mona to speak with Mohan. Ms. Gladia expressed to

A Bully's Disguise

Mohan that it may have been a bad idea for she and Mona to move to New York and that she would perhaps consider returning to Georgia. Mohan went quiet on the phone, as he turned and watched his grandmother's facial expression.

"Thank you, Ms. Gladia. Will Mona be able to attend school tomorrow?" asked Mohan.

"I cannot answer that question, right now. She is feeling better, but is still a bit shaken up by that horrible experience! She wants to go to school, so I will decide later. She wants to see you, too!" replied Ms. Gladia.

Mohan hung up the phone and prepared for bed. The house went to a silence, as Mohan walked with his grandmother to his room. Mohan knew that there were a number of things that he would need to contemplate, before returning to school.

Mohan got very little sleep that night. He spent much of the night tossing and turning. He worried about the welfare of his old friend, Mona. He wondered whether it was possible to convince his friends that Mona would be a great addition to their group. "Would Mona even want to be a part of the group, now?" Mohan pondered aloud. "How can I reassure her that PS 1102 is a great school with great people?" Finally, Mohan wondered whether Collette could really be responsible for the bee incident and, if so, what would make her act that way? Mohan clasped his hands and said his prayers. He lay on his bed with his hands clasped behind his head. Gazing at the ceiling, he hoped for a better day at school for Mona. Mohan was also looking forward to feeling better and returning to school.

Within a couple days, Mohan was physically ready to return to school. He had Grandma Celeste to thank for playing a key role in his recovery! While he was excited to head back to school, a sense of fear lingered in his mind. He felt the tickles of butterflies in his stomach, just like when he started PS 1102, a little more than a year ago.

Chapter 9 - Stand Up for Your Rights

It was a sunny Spring day and Mrs. Singh was attempting to pick out a pair of shorts, to match the short-sleeved t-shirt that Mohan would wear upon his return to school.

"Mom, do I really have to wear shorts? I don't like to wear shorts to school. Dad always said that school is a place to learn and boys should dress in long pants," said Mohan.

Mrs. Singh paused and stared at Mohan in shock. "How do you remember that?" she asked.

"I remember a lot of things that my dad told me. He is with me every day in my heart! I even speak to him when I need a man's opinion," replied Mohan, with a smile on his face.

A Bully's Disguise

Mrs. Singh looked very confused.

"Your father passed away a little while ago Mohan, it is nice to find that you remember so much about him," Mrs. Singh went on.

"Don't worry mom, I will never forget him!" Mohan exclaimed.

Mrs. Singh replaced Mohan's shorts with a pair of long pants and as Mohan dressed for school, Mrs. Singh thought of how much she avoided speaking to Mohan about his dad, so that he would not be saddened by the loss. She now realized that Mohan was old enough, even at nine years old, to know that his dad would never return, but that the memories of his dad, were fond ones.

"There, a perfectly dressed young schoolboy!" said Mohan, after dressing.

"I wish I could say the same thing when you return home after school, with your shirt out of your pants and stains on your clothes!" replied Mrs. Singh.

Mohan and Mrs. Singh hugged and laughed as they walked down the stairs and out the door for school. Grandma Celeste stopped Mohan for a quick hug and told him to remember her advice on his decision making at school. Mrs. Singh was not fully informed about Mona, since she had gotten home too late that night.

Everyone gathered in the auditorium and as Mohan walked in, his head was spinning round and round, looking for the little girl with the two pigtails. Walter ran up to Mohan and the two did their secret hand shake.

"Did you see your friend, Mona?" asked

Walter.

"Nah, where is she? I am still looking for her right now!" replied Mohan anxiously.

"Hey, you. Big head!" said a voice from behind.

It was Mona. She did not look the same.

Mona's hair looked different, no more pigtails. Mohan stood with his mouth open and watched Mona from head to toe.

"Wow, you look so different," Mohan said.

"So do you, tall boy," Mona replied.

Mohan's face changed as he looked at the swelling on her face from the bee stings. For a few seconds, the two old friends were in a world of their own, forgetting all the bad things that had happened to Mona, previously. Mohan suddenly leaned down and gave Mona a tight hug. Mona rested her head on his shoulder and wept a bit.

"We finally got to see each other! You are the brother that I never had," Mona said.

"You are the sister, I never had, as well!" Mohan replied.

"Okay, okay. Break up the water works here folks! We are in school. A place of fun and friends," said Walter.

Mona and Mohan laughed at Walter's comment and walked towards the class line.

Mohan noticed Joseph running breathlessly towards him.

"Welcome back, Mohan," he said.

"Hey, Collette's dad just dropped her off. She should be heading here in a few," whispered Joseph, trying to avoid Mona from hearing his comment.

A Bully's Disguise

Mona walked in front of Mohan and looked back every second to make sure he was behind.   Walter flipped his eyeballs in disgust.

"Do you have to babysit her all the time, now?" Walter asked.

"No, I do not plan to," Mohan replied.

"Let's go to the back of the line," said Joseph to Mohan and Walter.

As the three boys walked to the back of the line together, Mona got out of the line with a bright smile on her face, too.

"No way your tail is coming too, Mohan. Get rid of her," said Walter.

Mohan did not respond, since Mona was close enough to hear, if he did. Collette joined the line as they all walked to the third floor. Mohan did not look back to greet Collette, nor did she greet him. Usually, Collette would run up to Mohan and start to chat nonstop about something random, but that had not been the case for the past few weeks. It was still the silent treatment for Mohan.

Mohan thought of all the things his grandmother had said and remembered his father's advice, as well. He was ready to make this school day a good one for all, even if some of his friends got their feelings hurt. As the children sat to start the school day, Lulu came in and looked at Mohan with a smile. She whispered to him that the two of them would talk when they switched for Art class.

Strangely, Collette sat quietly with her head in her notebook. Walter leaned over to peek to see what she was drawing, then it dawned on him. Walter remembered Lulu's mentions of a drawing in the girl's bathroom, insulting Mona, on her first day. He sat back and thought of the only person, who started drawing compulsively, since Mohan mentioned Mona, a few weeks earlier. Walter froze in his seat.

During Art class, Ms. Trudy asked everyone to continue drawing and painting, as she sat at her desk. Lulu used the opportunity to sit next to Mohan to chat. She wanted to fill him in with all that had happened while he was absent. Lulu also reminded Mohan about her tenth birthday party, which she had coming up this same weekend.

"I gave the class those invitations about a month ago, so I do hope you asked your mom to bring you," Lulu said.

"Do I need to bring my chopsticks to this party?" asked Walter, with a grin on his face.

"Yes, Walter. Walk with a bib for your big mouth, too!" replied Lulu.

Mohan and LuLu laughed.

"You are not funny Lulu," said Walter.

"I was not trying to be, just stating facts Walter," said Lulu.

"Just because I'm Japanese, does not mean that my family and I only eat Japanese foods," went on Lulu.

"Look, I don't care what country the food is from, once it tastes good and there is meat, I am good! If you guys want to come to a jhandi one day, then you will learn to appreciate meat!" went on Mohan.

"I thought you told us that at a jhandi, there is no meat?" asked Walter, puzzled.

"That's my point! I love food, but prefer to eat meat as part of a meal. At a jhandi, there is no meat. I meant you appreciate meat even more, since it is not part of the meal!" said Mohan.

"Walter, why do we always need to explain everything to you in such great detail?" asked Lulu.

Ms. Trudy called out to Walter and told him to sit and stop leaning over to Mohan and Lulu's table.

Lulu never hesitated to speak her mind. She was very straightforward with Mohan and told him of her suspicions about Collette. She went on to tell Mohan that she strongly believed that Collette posted the flyer, with the awful drawing about Mona, in the girl's bathroom. Mohan exhaled, stopped painting, folded his hands and glanced over to Collette's table in the Art room. Collette didn't notice him, as she was busy painting.

"We will settle this thing, once and for all, in the school yard, after lunch," said Mohan.

"What's that suppose to mean?" asked Walter.

"I am tired of the tension that exists amongst us. When I started at this school, last year, it was very tough for me. Even Walter and Joseph gave me a hard time, but I realized that it was not about them testing my strengths, but it was more about, ME. Me being strong enough to put a stop to it," went on Mohan.

Walter called Joseph to tell him the plan for the school yard.

"I still think that we should tell the teacher or our parents before you address this,

A Bully's Disguise

Mohan," said Lulu.

Walter interjected....

"I neither agree for teachers nor parents to get involved! Some things are better solved by us," said Walter.

Ms. Trudy walked over and asked what had happened. She wanted to know why there was a huddle during her Art class. Lulu looked at Mohan in the eye and was tempted to say something, but did not.

Mona was busy doing her Art project as Collette and her new group of friends sat and whispered about Mona's work. Ms. Trudy observed what the girls were doing and separated them.

During lunch, Mohan and his friends rushed to finish their food. The boys hurried into the school yard to chat freely.

"Alright, this is how I feel. I am about to confront Collette about her behavior towards me and then steer the conversation towards the subject of Mona," said Mohan.

"Just understand, whatever happens in this school yard, must stay here. If I hear of anyone saying what happened, you will be called out as a snitch and be reviled," claimed Walter.

"No way! You don't make rules for anybody but yourself! Who died and made you king, Walter?" questioned Lulu.

"Yes, Walter. I agree with Lulu. I am not going to follow your lead," said Joseph.

Walter walked off to the bench, under the bee infested tree, and sat by himself. No one followed him, but he watched to see what would happen next.

A Bully's Disguise

Mohan ran alongside Collette as she walked around the track. She tried her best to avoid him, but Mohan was not allowing her to ignore him this time. He walked in front of her and said:

"I will have my mom call your mom and tell her of the things you did to Mona. I know it was you. If you do not speak to me now, I will tell on you," Mohan went on.

Collette grabbed Mohan's hand and pulled him to the side of the fence. Mohan was surprised by her actions.

"You will not do such a thing!" replied Collette with her teeth tightly clenched.

"I will too! I can't believe you would encourage her to go by that beehive and fan herself, to tease those bees!" said Mohan.

"You have to go to Mona and apologize,"

he added.

"I will never apologize!" Collette exclaimed. "It was her fault for moving here, anyway. It is not fair that she came and disrupted our friendship. All you ever talked about was how great it would be for Mona to be here!" continued Collette.

Mohan sighed. He did not realize that he had been making Collette feel left out; however, he needed to put an end to all of the tension and conflict that persisted.

"I'm really sorry for making you feel this way. I was just trying to help everyone get along. You're one of the best friends I've ever had and no one can change that. Mona is also a really good friend. I thought that all of us could be great friends, together," Mohan explained.

A Bully's Disguise

"If you want, we can put all of these problems behind us and move on," Mohan continued.

"First, we must all apologize to each other," he stated.

"I'll start. I'm really sorry for making you feel left out and I will try my best to be considerate of your feelings," Mohan promised.

"You should apologize to Mona," went on Mohan.

"I can't do that. She did not think it was me and besides, Mona likes me. I feel really bad to have misled her this way," Collette admitted.

"She will forgive you and we can all put this craziness behind us," said Mohan.

Lulu and Mona were coming toward

Anaya Lee Willabus

Collette and Mohan, with Ms. Anita a few paces behind. Walter jumped up from the bench and Joseph stopped playing basketball.

Ms. Anita approached the children and asked what had transpired. Finally, Collette said that she wanted to have her mother visit the school, to have a sit down, and to talk about what was revealed.

Ms. Anita took Mona, Collette, Mohan, Lulu, Joseph and Walter to Mr. Bartfort's office. After a few minutes of chatting with the children, Mr. Bartfort arranged for the children's parents to have a meeting at the school with him. He wanted to ensure that the group had resolved any conflicts and he wished to have a discussion on the school's policy on bullying. Finally, he wanted to talk about the best ways to handle and resolve future conflicts. Mr. Bartfort went on to explain that there was a no tolerance policy in the school, for anyone bullying another child. He made it clear that if any of the students were to attempt such an act again, that child or children, would be suspended!

Mohan and his classmates were scared out of their wits. Everyone went quiet and even Collette looked remorseful for her actions. Mr. Bartfort did commend the group for being mature enough to address their problems and willingness to work towards improving their relationship.

Chapter 10 - Forgive and Forget

The next day, the children's parents visited the school, to discuss, for the first time, the tangled mess between friends.

Mr. Bartfort explained, what he expected of the children, to their parents and the children agreed to comply with the rules.

"Well, at least we were able to iron out this confusion, so that we can continue to go to the school yard and play," said Mohan.

"Before all of you start to run out of here, don't forget my birthday party on Saturday," said LuLu. "I'd hate to have to use some of the new moves I learned from my karate class, on you guys, for missing my party!" chuckled Lulu.

"You know, very well, sensei told us to

represent ourselves, only if it is necessary!" replied Mohan.

"If you miss my party, it would be very necessary to represent myself," laughed Lulu.

The whole group laughed at LuLu's comments.

"Mona, I didn't send you an invitation because you were not yet here when I gave them out," went on Lulu.

"Don't worry about it, once you are okay with her coming, I will tell her mom about it," replied Mohan.

"So, will we see some Kung Fu at this party, or what?" asked Walter, with his usual silly face on.

"I refuse to answer you," said Lulu.

"It is Shotokan Karate that Lulu and I practice," interjected Mohan. "It originated in

Japan. Take Walter's invitation and give it to Mona," said Mohan, jokingly.

Mona was so happy to be around Mohan that she was willing to forgive Collette and move on. She was also interested in learning more about her new school, new friends and life in New York. Collette kept quiet and walked shyly back to class with the others. Principal Bartfort stood at the door of his office with his hands folded and listened to the children as they walked to their classroom. The conversation switched to Lulu's birthday.

Mona caught up to Collette and asked if they could start over as new friends. Collette smiled and nodded, yes. Their conversation quickly shifted to what would be a good gift for Lulu and what outfits would be worn to the party.

A Bully's Disguise

As the weekend drew closer, the children looked forward to celebrating with good food and good friends.

As the children walked, Mohan thought to himself that fourth grade did not seem so tough after all!

It seemed as though, the children had each other and the support from their family and school to overcome life's unexpected hurdles.

Check out Anaya Lee Willabus' other book:

'The Day Mohan Found His Confidence'

About the Author

Anaya Lee Willabus is a nine year old, award winning author and poet.

She started reading at age two and continues to challenge herself by reading various genres of books.

Anaya aspires to continue her career as an accomplished author, as well as, working towards the goals of becoming a world class athlete and teacher.

This book sheds light on Anaya's versatile writing skills, by continuing to provide insight into the life of the character Mohan.

Children can learn valuable lessons on friendship, self respect and the challenges of growing up, after reading this book.

Check out Anaya's other book:

   *'**The Day Mohan Found His Confidence**.'*

Made in the USA
Middletown, DE
16 June 2016